WHAT A HANDSOME BOY I AM

BY SHAKIA DAVIS

ILLUSTRATED BY FEDERICO A. FRANZESE

www.mannishbyshakia.com

DEDICATION

For as long as I can remember, I have always wanted to be a mother. In my wildest dreams, I saw myself being the mother of two fascinating little boys that would one day grow up to be phenomenal men. This has not yet happened in my life, but I have acquired a league of male friends and their sons which have become like brothers and nephews to me. Over the years, these men have opened up to me to discuss their fears, triumphs, and insecurities and every day I find myself in a constant state of awe. My love and respect for men is endless and I wish to encourage and inspire men in their greatness in any way possible. With this book, I hope to help encourage and inspire the future generation of men by starting the cycle of love and encouragement while the reader is still young and life has not yet begun to infiltrate his thinking with false truths.

To men, to my guys (my friends and family), to little boys all around the world, and most importantly to the sons of my wildest dreams - I dedicate this to you.

What a handsome boy I am.

My teeth shine as bright as the twinkle of the stars.

What a handsome boy I am.

My skin is dark like the night sky that seems so far.

What a handsome boy I am.

My nose is wide like the pharaohs of old,

What a handsome boy I am.

And my sense of style is unique, unmatched, and bold.

What a handsome boy I am.

Because of my looks, some people don't like me–

What a handsome boy I am.

Sometimes it hurts my feelings but my inner star still shines on so brightly.

What a handsome boy I am.

"How can he be so calm and cool?" I hear friends say,

What a handsome boy I am.

The secret is that royalty is in my DNA.

What a handsome boy I am.

See, my hair grows towards the sun and rests on my head like a crown,

What a handsome boy I am.

And serves as a constant reminder whenever I'm feeling down

What a handsome boy I am.

That I should not give energy to words that are hurtful and mean

What a handsome boy I am.

Because I am a young prince that will one day grow into a king

What a handsome boy I am.

So, until that day, I will always take pride

What a handsome boy I am.

In how I look, how I treat others, and my good heart inside.

What a handsome boy I am.

I will always find my happiness whenever I'm in a jam

What a handsome boy I am.

Because I know, and will never forget, what a handsome boy I am.

ABOUT THE AUTHOR

Shakia Davis is a menswear wardrobe stylist and consultant and author of the new children's book What A Handsome Boy I Am. As a menswear stylist, Shakia has spent a great deal of time building relationships with men from various backgrounds and cultures and has helped to groom their outer appearance in conjunction with being instrumental in helping to develop their inner workings as well. Shakia has a Bachelor of Arts degree in Communication from Coastal Carolina University where she began her career as a stylist by freelancing in order to help fellow colleagues overcome fashion challenges and encourage social and personal development. Shakia's motto for the men she styles is "focus on the details," a motto she has adopted in her everyday life. For the rest of her life.

Made in the USA
Middletown, DE
28 February 2021